MAGNA COW

Written by Barry Hutchison

Illustrated by Cate James

Brisket was not like the other cows in her field.
Her horns were curlier. Her tail was frizzier.
And she glowed faintly in the dark.

This book
belongs to:

....

....

....

For Alan and Susan, who saw something amoosing in this little cow's tale – BH

For Hemel – CJ

Special thanks to Chloe, Kevin, Dave and Paul – LDB

Published by Little Door Books 2018
This edition published 2018
ISBN: 978-0-9927520-6-4
Text copyright © Barry Hutchison 2018
Illustrations copyright © Cate James 2018

Little Door Books
mail@littledoorbooks.co.uk
www.littledoorbooks.co.uk
twitter: @littledoorbooks

But everyone was asleep by then, so no one ever noticed.

Even stranger, Brisket was magnetic, so metal things would stick to her with a...

KAAALUNK!

Some cows thought it was magic.
Others blamed it on bad luck.
Or that time she ate all the magnets on the farmer's fridge door.

But no one knew for sure,
because cows have no real understanding of science.

Brisket tried hard to fit in with the rest of the herd.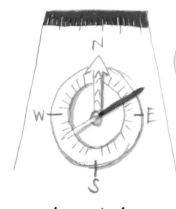

She loved going on camping trips
to the North Field.

But her magnetic powers

made the compass go all WONKY

and they got completely...

...LOST!

And when they finally made it to the campsite,

SOMEONE

pulled out all the tent pegs.

She helped build
the big treehouse.

But then, KAAALUNK! she got too close and all the nails flew out, and the whole thing tumbled to the ground with a

CRASH!

By the time the Moove to the Moosic dance contest came around, the other cows had had enough.

"We've spent weeks making this fancy trophy," said Gertrude.

"And we don't want you spoiling it," agreed Muriel. "So stay out of our way."

Brisket was sent to stand at the top of the hill, alone. All she could do was watch, occasionally doing a sad little hoof shuffle and flicking her tail in time to the music.

The other cows danced and jigged, frolicked and flipped,

bounced and boogied, their hooves pounding the grass like thunder.

As they danced the hill shuddered and the old tractor began to tremble. Slowly at first, then faster and faster, it began to roll. Down, down, down the hill it trundled, heading straight for the fancy trophy!

The other cows were too busy strutting their stuff to notice.

"LOOK OUT!" Brisket bellowed.

But the music was too loud and the beat was too funky, and nobody heard her cry.

"Somebody do something!" she wailed.
Brisket looked around the empty hilltop.

"OH, COW PATS," she said.

"Looks like it's up to me!"

Brisket focused all her magnetic
powers and tried to heave the
tractor back, but it was too heavy.
The tractor wasn't going to stop.

The fancy trophy was going to be SQUISHED!

At the bottom of the hill, the dancing cows
finally spotted the runaway tractor.

"Oh no, the fancy trophy!" they cried.
"I can't look!" said Great Aunt Daisy,
covering her eyes with her hooves.

But a split second before it turned the fancy trophy into scrap, the tractor shuddered, and wobbled, and fell to pieces with a...

KAAALUNK!

And there, covered from horns to hoof in bolts and bits was... BRISKET.

The cows CHEERED.

"You saved the fancy trophy!" cried Getrude.

"With your magic!" cried Muriel, because cows still had no real understanding of science.

"You're our hero!" they told her.
"Our superhero!"
"Our very own

MAGNA COW!"

Brisket and all her friends danced and laughed together until the cows came home.

And she never accidentally spoiled their fun again. Well...

...almost never.